The Hunter

Published by Spines
ISBN: 979-8-89691-003-9

The Hunter

AND OTHER SHORT STORIES

CLEONIES ODOM

Contents

Dedication

This book is dedicated to the many personalities and experiences that made it possible.

The Hunter

As if summoned by some unseen force, the band began to sing in his headphones, "... You don't know my mind. You don't know my kind. Dark necessities are part of my design." He wasn't sure what it meant, but he knew what it meant to him. Dark Necessities by the Red-Hot Chili Peppers had become his theme song. Its dark, mysterious message and hypnotic rhythm had become the soundtrack to his grizzly nightly activities. In the dimly lit kitchen of a small, aging house, crouched a young boy named Ethan. His movements were methodical, practiced, and stealthy. His eyes scanned every crack and crevice with an intensity far beyond his years. Ethan was only nine, but the shadows in his eyes and the heaviness in his heart made him seem much older.

His parents, oblivious to his actions, often fought

behind closed doors, their angry voices seeping through the walls and poisoning the air like some gaseous cloud. Their neglect had carved a chasm deep in Ethan's soul, one that he filled with an obsession born from loneliness, anger, and his darkest fantasies.

Ethan had become a predator. The kitchen was his hunting ground, and cockroaches were his prey. He knew every corner, every hiding spot where the roaches sought refuge. His fingers twitched with anticipation. His eyes sparkled as he closed in on his first target of the night. With a swift, practiced motion, he captured the unsuspecting insect, its tiny legs thrashing in vain against his grip.

His young, innocent-looking face remained emotionless as he laid the cockroach on the wooden board he had repurposed for his grim activities. Methodically, he began to pull off its legs, one by one, watching intently as the creature 's antennae moved swiftly back and forth! It's only expression of obvious agony. Each leg was a fragment of his fractured psyche, and each pull brought a twisted sense of control.

With all its legs removed, the cockroach was a pitiful, helpless being, much like Ethan felt inside. Yet, his tortuous deeds didn't end there. He reached for a thin, rusted nail and carefully impaled the legless insect onto the board. The sight of its futile squirming provided a momentary solace to his inner chaos.

But Ethan's most sadistic ritual was yet to come. He turned towards the stove, its cold metal surface reflecting his hollow gaze. He twisted the knob, igniting a small flame that licked the edges of the red-hot eyelet. The heat radiated off it, distorting the air around it in a shimmering haze.

With careful precision, Ethan lifted the board, carrying the impaled cockroach towards the stove. He held it above the scorching eyelet, feeling the heat rise and prickle his skin. Then, with a deliberate motion, he placed the legless roach onto the burning metal.

The insect's body convulsed in agony, a silent scream emanating from its tiny form. Ethan watched, entranced, as the cockroach's exoskeleton began to char and crackle. The smell of burning flesh mingled with the stagnant air, creating an acrid scent that filled the kitchen.

In those moments, Ethan felt a dark satisfaction, a release from the torment that gnawed at his heart. The suffering of the cockroach mirrored his own, yet it also gave him a twisted sense of power over the pain that consumed him.

As the insect's movements ceased and its body lay still, Ethan's moment of reprieve faded. The darkness inside him remained an insidious presence that could not be purged by his sadistic acts. He knew that his actions were wrong and that they only deepened the chasm within him. But in his young, tormented mind, it was the only way he knew to cope with the emotional storm that raged inside.

The cycle would continue, each night bringing a new hunt, a new victim to suffer under his merciless hands. Ethan was trapped in a web of his own making, a fragile boy lost in the dark maze of his mind, searching for a way out that he could not find.

The January Man

Sitting by the window, Margaret stared at the barren, frost-covered landscape. The wind howled, and the skeletal trees bowed beneath its cold, relentless force. Her breath fogged the glass, tracing delicate patterns across the surface. The world outside was dormant, paralyzed by winter's icy grip, but her heart beat violently within her chest, alive with a love she knew was too dangerous to speak of aloud.

The man she loved was broken. Alec had always been an enigma—quiet, distant, yet impossibly magnetic. When she first met him in the dim, smoke-filled bar on the edge of town about a year ago, he was already a ghost of a man. His eyes, a pale blue like the frigid winter skies, seemed to look through her as if she were some inanimate, transparent specter. And yet, despite the darkness that clouded his soul, something about him made him impossible to resist. It wasn't his beauty that captured her, though Alec was handsome in a sharp, rugged, outdoorsy kind of way. His face seemed chiseled by suffering, and something about the scars beneath his calm surface called to the deepest part of her. The mystery of his pain was intoxicating, and Margaret—once so sure of herself—felt lost whenever she was near him.

The first time she kissed him, it had been in a storm. The heavens had opened above them, rain drenching their bodies as they stood on the stone steps of his old, crumbling mansion at the edge of town. She had been the one to press her lips to his despite the cold look in his eyes, despite the warnings everyone had given her. He had kissed her back but with a desperation that tasted more like sorrow than desire.

"You don't want me," he whispered, his breath hot and moist against her neck. "Trust me. You don't know me." But Margaret, foolish in her love, had only smiled. "I'll be the judge of that." she said. She had no idea how truthful his words were. As the days turned into weeks and the weeks into months, the more of him she saw, the more of him she wanted to see. Yet the more she tried to reach him, the more he seemed to retreat, hiding deep within himself. There were moments when he would pull her close, his hands gripping her like a man desperately trying to escape some unseen danger.

But then, without warning, he would grow cold again, hiding in the foggy shadows of his mind where she could not follow. Margaret had heard disturbing rumors whispered through the town like some frightening ancient myth. The tale of Alec's past and a possible link to some missing women, though no one seemed to know all the details, was the kind of stuff you only see in movies or read about. He'd grown up in Cutlerville but moved away after college.

After being away for more than twenty years, he was back. Official-looking men in dark suits with badges followed, asking strange questions about a group of local women who'd become known affectionately as the C-20. The C-20 or Cutlerville 20 was a group of young college-aged women who'd gone missing during the month of January back in 2003 without a trace. Their freshly dumped bodies were discovered by law enforcement that following January more than twenty years ago.

It seemed women had gone missing everywhere Alec had been. Police noticed a pattern. They observed that the women began to disappear around January in each location spanning some 20 years and that the disappearances stopped around January of each following year. Because of this pattern, F.B.I. profilers called their suspect "The January Man."

A wealth of regret

Harrison Crutchfield sat quietly in his office gazing out at the large, recumbent estate he now called home. He traced the treetops with his eyes as they swayed gently in the wind, but his thoughts were in times gone by. They traveled back to when his child—Lauren, was still in his life when laughter and love filled his home. But those days were distant now, stolen away by the lies of her mother, Karen.

Karen had left him two decades ago, not for another man but for a woman. Her coming out had shattered their marriage, but it wasn't that which hurt him the most. What broke him was the way she poisoned Lauren against him, weaving a web of deceit that painted him as a cruel, selfish man who had abandoned her. Repeatedly, he tried to reach her, desperate to explain his side of the story,but her heart had grown cold.

As the years drifted by, Birthdays and holidays were spent alone. Eventually, he realized he was indeed cut off. In Lauren's mind, he had become nothing more than a deadbeat, a loser who didn't deserve her time or affection. She never seemed to realize he loved her more than anything, and that he had worked tirelessly to support her despite his many financial setbacks.

But that was in the past now! Life had taken a surprising turn for him in those lonely years. He found solace in writing; his pain poured into novels that captivated millions. Before long, he was not just successful; he'd become one of the wealthiest authors in the country. His books, filled with themes of loss, betrayal, and redemption, resonated with readers far and wide. He had also become a quiet philanthropist, using his newfound wealth to support causes close to his heart.

Yet, despite all his success, Lauren remained absent from his life. Not one call. Not a single text.

He often wondered if she even knew who he had become. Did she read his books without realizing the author was her father? Did she drive past billboards with his name and shrug, assuming it was someone else?

Now, as he felt the weight of time pressing on his shoulders, Harrison knew his journey was nearing its end. His body was failing him, even though his mind remained sharp. He'd had years to plan for this, and as the final chapters of his life played out, he made sure every detail was in place. His estate, vast beyond imagination, would be left to his only child. It was Harrison's final act of love, a gesture that he hoped would bridge the gaps left behind by bitterness and lies.

The letter came as a shock.

Lauren and her fiance` had just setteled in for the evening when she opened the certified letter. It had sat unopened on the kitchen counter for a few days. She was just about to toss it into the trash, but decided to open it out of curiosity. It informed her of the death of her father and that she was invited to the reading of his will. "What", she asked. A wave of remorse washed over her. She always planned to reconnect with him, but it simply hadn't been a priority. It was now too late. Tears formed in her eyes flowing down her chin. She was now sobbing uncontrollably. The letter went on to say that the reading would be the following Tuesday at the office of the attorney.

Tuesday finally came. The days after learning of her father's death seem to creep by deepening her agony. She couldn't help but wonder how her father was able to afford an attorney like this or who was paying the bill. As she sat down, the lawyer unfurled the details of the will, Her head spun. her father, it turned out, had become incredibly wealthy and was one of the most successful authors in the world. His estates, bank accounts, and investments were valued in the hundreds of millions of dollars. She sat in stunned silence as the news sank in—she was to inherit a fortune from a man she had dismissed as a looser.

Her mind raced back to all the years she'd dismissed him, assumed he was struggling, assumed he was a failure. She couldn't reconcile the image of the penniless father she'd carried in her mind with the philanthropist and author the lawyer described.

"How is this possible?" she muttered, almost to herself.

The lawyer's expression remained neutral. "Your father led a very private life, especially after he stopped hearing from you." He hesitated before adding, "He never spoke ill of you. Not once."

Shame and regret washed over her, drowning her in memories of the many times she'd given her father the cold shoulders and ignored his text messages. Her mother had convinced her years ago that her father was a selfish man, that he had abandoned her for his own interests. She now realized how incredibly different reality was.

Lauren stood, unable to sit still any longer. "I turned my back on him.

Overwhelmed by guilt, her voice began to crack as tears streamed from her eyes once more. Nothing could excuse or justify her icy indifference.

The attorney placed a small box on the table, sliding it toward her. "There is one last thing," he said. "Your father wrote a letter for you. He wanted you to have it after his passing."

Inside the box was a neatly folded envelope. She stared at it reluctantly afraid of what it might say.

When she finally opened the letter, tears flooded her eyes. There was no trace of bitterness or admonition. Instead, it was filled with fatherly love. He told herhow proud he was, how he had followed her life from afar, and how much he wanted her to cherish life and to never take one another for granted. He said despite the hurt, he had never stopped loving her.

"You were always in my heart," the letter concluded.

As she read her father's words, the heavy weight of her choices became unbearable as the realization that she had allowed her father to die without ever trying to give him the benefit of the doubt or even reconnect with him caused an eruption of sobs and grief! And now, all she had left were his words, his wealth, and a haunting regret that could never be undone.

But maybe, in this final act, there was also a glimmer of hope—a chance to forgive herself and remember the man who had always loved her unconditionally, even when she hadn't loved him back.

A New Perception

In the year 2266, humanity was on the brink of a technological renaissance, with advancements in artificial intelligence, space travel, and biogenetics shaping a rapidly evolving world. However, nothing could have prepared Earth for what was about to unfold.

It was a clear, sunny day in Lagos, Nigeria, when the sky seemed to shimmer and tear apart, revealing a vessel unlike anything ever seen on Earth or conceived by the human mind. It was an ethereal, translucent, radiant structure resembling a cosmic web of light and energy. The craft floated silently, undetected by satellites or radar, a testament to technology thousands of light years ahead of Earth's capabilities.

Global military forces scrambled, their jets and drones made obsolete by the sheer presence of the alien craft. World leaders convened emergency meetings, struggling to comprehend and respond to this unprecedented event. The anticipation and tension were palpable as every eye on the planet turned towards Nigeria, the unexpected epicenter of this momentous occasion.

Across the globe, screens flickered to life, broadcasting the surreal scene. In the heart of Lagos, crowds gathered, their faces a mixture of awe and trepidation. News anchors whispered hurried commentary, their voices quivering with a blend of fear and excitement. Humanity held its collective breath as a section of the alien craft began to descend, forming a graceful ramp to the ground.

From the ship appeared beings of striking beauty and elegance. They were tall, their skin a deep, lustrous black that seemed to absorb and reflect the sunlight in a mesmerizing dance of hues. Their features were majestic, their eyes holding an ancient wisdom and kindness that transcended human understanding. Dressed in flowing garments that shimmered like liquid metal, they walked with a grace that was both alien and familiar.

The world watched in stunned silence as the aliens approached the gathered crowd. One of the beings stepped forward, a figure of commanding presence and serene dignity. She raised a hand, and a harmonious tone resonated through the air, instantly translated into every known language.

"People of Earth," she began, her voice carrying a melodic resonance that echoed across continents. "We come in peace. We are the Akin, travelers of the cosmos, and we have long observed your world with compassion and interest."

The crowd in Lagos, and indeed the world, remained entranced as she continued. "Black people of Earth, we are your brothers and sisters. Our journey has brought us back to our ancestral kin. You are the descendants of a great lineage, a heritage that extends beyond the stars."

As her words sank in, the implications rippled through the fabric of human society. Centuries of prejudice and systemic racism were laid bare. The falsehoods and injustices starkly contrasted against the revelation of shared cosmic ancestry. The realization struck with the force of a seismic shift, reshaping beliefs and shattering the foundations of bigotry.

In the streets of Lagos, there was a mixture of celebration and solemn reflection. Across the world, people of African descent stood a little taller, their pride and dignity reaffirmed by this cosmic kinship. For others, there was a moment of profound reckoning, a call to introspection and change.

The Akin spent days among the people of Earth,

sharing knowledge, healing the sick, and fostering a new sense of unity and purpose. They spoke of the interconnectedness of all life, the importance of harmony and respect, and the boundless potential that lay within humanity.

As they prepared to depart, the Akin left behind a beacon of hope and a promise of continued friendship. They ascended back into their ship, which shimmered and faded from sight, leaving the world forever changed.

In the years that followed, humanity embarked on a journey of transformation. Nations worked together to dismantle systems of oppression and inequality, inspired by the visit of their cosmic brethren. Scientific and cultural advancements flourished in an era marked by cooperation and mutual respect.

The year 2266 would be remembered as the dawn of a new epoch, a time when the people of Earth looked to the stars and saw not just the vastness of the universe, but a reflection of their own potential for greatness. The message of the Akin resonated through generations, a testament to the enduring power of unity and the boundless reach of human and cosmic kinship.

A Pain Like No Other

❧

J ames sat in the hallway of his parents' home. His mind wandered as he stared deep into nothing-ness. This was his way of finding the "I". The "I" was his term for inspiration or the spark that ignited the creativity of his mind. He was a gentle soul with a passion for storytelling. He often spent his days weaving intricate tales, dreaming of one day becoming a renowned author. However, his family never under-stood his passion or accepted his dream. They were practical folk, believing in steady jobs and reliable incomes. They considered James shiftless and a dreamer at best.

Knock, Knock! "Get up in there!" It was James's dad, Alvin. He got up every morning at 5 am without exception and expected everyone else to do the same. He couldn't stand it that James liked books and often complained that James was not a "man's man". Tom, James's younger brother was a lot like their dad. He worked a steady job as a construction worker, but work had been slow due to the weather. He'd been up about 30 minutes already and was eating his favorite cereal when James finally made his way down the rickety stairs. Their mother Peggy was just getting out of bed. She was a quiet unassuming woman who pretty much went along with whatever her husband said to avoid confrontation. So, when an incident occurred that changed James's life forever. She sided with her husband.

James's younger brother, Tom, was caught stealing money from their parents. In a desperate attempt to escape punishment, Tom pointed the finger at James, claiming that James had coerced him into stealing. James vehemently denied the accusation, but his family chose to believe Tom. They saw James's imaginative nature and love for fiction as evidence of his capacity for deceit.

Heartbroken and disowned by his family, James left home with nothing but a few belongings and his notebook. He wandered from town to town, doing odd jobs to survive. Despite the harshness of his circumstances, he never stopped writing. His stories became his solace, his escape from the pain of rejection.

Years passed, and James's perseverance paid off. His

unique voice and compelling narratives caught the attention of a prominent literary agent. His first book, "Echoes of a Shattered Heart," was published to critical acclaim, and soon, James became a household name. His subsequent novels solidified his status as one of the greatest authors of his generation. Fame and fortune followed, but James never forgot the pain of his family's betrayal.

One day, as James sat in his luxurious apartment in New York City, he received an unexpected phone call. It was Peggy, his mother. Her voice trembled as she spoke, filled with a mix of guilt and longing.

"James, it's your mother. We... we saw you on television. We read your books. We're so proud of you. We miss you. Can we... can we meet?"

His heart ached. The wounds of the past were still raw, but he had always longed for his family's love and acceptance. He agreed to meet them.

The reunion took place in a quaint café in the town where James grew up. As he walked in, memories of his childhood flooded back. His parents and siblings were already there, looking nervous and remorseful. His father, who had always been stern, was the first to speak.

"James, we were wrong. We should have believed you. Can you ever forgive us?"

James looked at their faces, seeing their sincerity

and regret. He took a deep breath, feeling a mix of anger, sadness, and relief. "I forgive you," he said softly. "But forgiveness doesn't mean forgetting. We have a lot to rebuild if we're going to move forward."

His family nodded, tears in their eyes. They spent the afternoon talking, reminiscing about the good times, and discussing their hopes for the future. It wasn't easy, but it was a start.

Over the next few years, James and his family worked hard to rebuild their relationship. It was a journey filled with ups and downs, but their shared desire for reconciliation kept them moving forward. James's fame continued to grow, but what mattered most to him was the mending of his family ties.

In the end, James's story wasn't just one of personal triumph and literary success, but also one of forgiveness and the power of second chances. His books continued to inspire millions, but his greatest achievement was the restoration of the family he had once lost.

Crash

Eight-year-old Lucas and his six-year-old sister, Emily, could hardly contain their excitement as they packed their overnight bags. They were spending the night with their aunt and uncle, something they had been looking forward to for weeks. Their parents, Mark and Sarah, had promised to take advantage of the child-free night to enjoy a rare dinner date, an opportunity for much-needed relaxation.

Lucas and Emily chattered excitedly during the car ride to their relatives' house. They planned games to play, and stories to tell, and were particularly excited about the promise of making s'mores around the fire pit. Mark and Sarah exchanged loving smiles, happy to see their children so thrilled.

After an enthusiastic welcome from Aunt Judy

and Uncle Tom, Lucas and Emily waved goodbye to their parents, who promised to pick them up the next morning. As the car drove away, Sarah glanced back at her children, her heart warmed by their happiness.

The evening passed in a whirl of fun. Lucas and Emily helped make pizza, played hide-and-seek, and finally gathered around the fire pit with their aunt and uncle. Laughter filled the air as they roasted marshmallows and made sticky s'mores. Exhausted but happy, the children eventually settled into their sleeping bags in the cozy guest room.

In the early hours of the morning, just as dawn's light began to creep into the sky, Aunt Judy's phone rang. She answered it groggily, not expecting anything more than a spam call at this hour. Instead, she was met with the urgent voice of a hospital nurse, relaying the devastating news: Mark and Sarah had been involved in a severe car crash.

Judy's heart pounded as she absorbed the details. The car had collided with a large truck on the highway. Mark had sustained minor injuries, but Sarah was in critical condition, fighting for her life. The nurse explained that Mark had requested Judy come to the hospital at once.

Judy took a deep breath, trying to steady herself. She glanced at the sleeping forms of Lucas and Emily, their innocent faces untroubled by the chaos unfolding. She woke Tom gently, explaining the situation in hushed tones. Tom immediately began to get dressed, preparing to drive Judy to the hospital.

Judy and Tom agreed not to wake the children just yet. They would wait until they had more information before breaking the news to them. Judy kissed the children on their foreheads before leaving, silently promising to do everything she could to help their family.

The hospital was a flurry of activity, with doctors and nurses rushing to and fro. Judy and Tom found Mark in the waiting area, his face pale and drawn. He looked up as they approached, his eyes filled with a mix of fear and relief.

"Sarah's in surgery," Mark said, his voice trembling. "They said it could be hours before we know anything."

Judy hugged her brother tightly, her own fear threatening to overwhelm her. They sat together, trying to offer each other comfort, as the hours ticked by painfully slowly.

Back at the house, Lucas and Emily awoke to find their aunt and uncle gone. They wandered into the kitchen, where their older cousin, Mia, was preparing breakfast. She had been woken early and filled in by her parents before they left, tasked with keeping the children distracted.

"Where's Aunt Judy and Uncle Tom?" Lucas asked, rubbing his eyes sleepily.

"They had to run an errand," Mia said gently, forcing a smile. "They'll be back soon. How about some pancakes?"

The children's curiosity was piqued but they were quickly distracted by the promise of their favorite breakfast. As they ate, Mia kept the conversation light, talking about plans for the day, hoping to keep their minds occupied.

Meanwhile, at the hospital, the wait seemed endless. Finally, a doctor approached them, her expression grave but not without hope.

"Mrs. Adams is out of surgery," she said. "She's stable, but it's still very critical. The next 24 hours are crucial."

Mark nodded, his grip tightening on Judy's hand. Relief mingled with dread as they prepared for the long vigil ahead.

Back at the house, Mia decided to take Lucas and Emily to the park, hoping the fresh air and playtime would keep them distracted. As they ran around, laughing and playing, the shadow of the morning's news hung heavily over Mia.

When Judy and Tom returned later that afternoon, they found the children still blissfully unaware.

They gathered everyone together in the living room, their expressions serious but calm.

"Lucas, Emily," Judy began gently, "we need to talk about something important."

The children's eyes widened with worry and anticipation as they listened. Judy and Tom explained what had happened, reassuring them that their dad was okay, and their mom was getting the best care possible.

"Can we see them?" Emily asked, her voice trembling.

"Not right now," Tom said softly. "But we'll go as soon as we can, and we'll make sure they know you're thinking of them."

The following days were a blur of hospital visits and anxious waiting. Lucas and Emily were finally able to see their father, who hugged them tightly, his eyes filled with tears. Sarah remained in intensive care, but there were small signs of improvement each day.

With the support of their family, the children found strength they didn't know they had. They drew pictures for their mom, wrote letters, and looked forward to the day she would wake up and come home.

Weeks later, Sarah finally opened her eyes. It was a slow, painful recovery, but surrounded by her family's love, she grew stronger each day. Lucas and Emily never left her side, their innocent faith a beacon of hope through the darkest times.

Ultimately, the family's bond was stronger than ever, forged through the fire of tragedy and adversity. They had faced a nightmare and emerged on the other side, their love a testament to the power of hope and resilience.

Desmond's End

"Ah!" he moaned as his body only moments ago, healthy, and athletic, now lay bloodied, broken, and trapped in the wreckage of his prized Mercedes SLS AMG. Having missed a tight hairpin turn, he'd collided with a large oak tree at 98 miles per hour in the middle of a moonless night on a lonely country road. "Help!" he yelled over and repeatedly, hoping somehow someone would hear his cries. But there was no one. As he lay bleeding, broken, and alone, shadows fell, and gray surrendered to black. As he left his home hours earlier, Desmond had no way of knowing how significant this day would be or that it would be both a farewell and an introduction.

It would be a farewell to a life in which he'd grown accustomed to being treated like a god since his exceptional, natural athletic abilities were discovered many years ago while playing on his middle school football team, but it would also be an introduction to a terrifying new reality; a reality from which he could never escape.

He was used to being catered to and loved being the center of attention. By the time he won the Heisman Trophy, his rugged good looks, along with his ripped 6'8 frame and magnetic, charismatic personality, had transformed Desmond "The Real" Deale into a Bonafide superstar before ever stepping onto an NFL field, and he knew it! In his mind, he was king. The world was his court and everyone in it was his subjects. For Desmond, being a superstar meant never apologizing for anything he said or did. When necessary, he simply turned on the charm.

But this was different; quite different! There were no adoring fans or groupies willing to do anything just to be in his presence. Darkness surrounded him. There was no moon glowing or stars twinkling against an opaqued sky. "Where am I?" he wondered. Not knowing what else to do, he yelled for help like never before! Fear set in as he began to hear blood-curdling screams in the distance. Pleas for mercy and forgiveness went unanswered. Then it hit him. He wasn't trapped in his car anymore. His body seemed different. Something prevented him from moving, but whatever it was, wasn't visible. "What is this?" he asked as he whimpered. Unable to move his neck, his eyes shifted from side to side and around. Sensing he was not alone, he begged, "Hello?" His invisible restraints loosened. As he began to sit up, he was grabbed by some malevolent entity with a stench so overwhelming he passed out. The feeling of his body being hurled into an abyss jolted him awake. As his body floated downward, the screams grew louder. He stumbled through the darkness, his eyes straining to see, but the void swallowed everything. A scream formed in his throat, but terror is a cruel, heartless thief.

The ground beneath him shifted, turning hot and jagged. Each step sent searing pain through his feet, but there was no other path. The air thickened, stinking of sulfur and decay, burning his lungs with every deliberate breath. He tried to cry out, to call for help, but the sound died in his throat, a hollow echo in the emptiness.

Suddenly, an ear-bursting cacophony of wails erupted around him, an unending orchestra of misery and pain. Specters of lost souls writhed in torment; their faces twisted in perpetual screams. Their eyes, hollow and black, locked onto Desmond, their pain seeping into his very being. He fell to his knees, clutching his head as their anguish became his own.

Memories of his life flooded his mind, each tainted with regret and remorse. He saw himself as careless and self-absorbed, hurting those who had loved him. He remembered the hurt in his wife's eyes the night he walked out, the tears of his children as he turned his back. Regret gnawed at him, a relentless beast that feasted on his soul. He screamed, but the darkness swallowed the sound, leaving only silence.

As the ground split open beneath him, he plummeted into a river of molten fire. The surface of his soul blistered and peeled away, exposing raw nerves to the searing heat. He thrashed and writhed, desperate to escape, but the flames only tightened their destructive grip. The agony was indescribable, an unending torture that consumed every fiber of his being.

As the flames licked his soul, grotesque figures emerged from the shadows, their eyes gleaming with malignant delight. They were the demons of his past, the monsters he had created with his own actions. They circled him, their laughter a cruel mockery. Each one took a turn, lashing him with fiery whips, their touch leaving searing brands on his soul.

He begged for mercy, but his pleas fell on the deafest ears. There was no redemption here, no solace in this abyss. The demons' laughter grew louder, drowning out his cries. They tore at him, ripping his soul, gnawing on his bones. His mind shattered under the relentless torment, but still, death refused him.

The darkness closed in around him, a suffocating

shroud pressing down on his chest. His screams became hoarse, a mere whisper in the void. The faces of those he had wronged danced before his eyes, their expressions twisted in pain and sorrow. He reached out to them, but they melted away, leaving him alone in his suffering.

In the end, there was only darkness and silence. Desmond's soul, broken and tormented, drifted in the endless void. The regret and remorse continued to devour him. This was the worm that would not die. There was no escape, no end to the torment. In this place of despair, he was doomed to suffer for all eternity, his screams echoing in the emptiness, unheard and unanswered.

Finally, Enough

Paul sat alone, quiet, and still. Plunk. An empty beer bottle slipped from his relaxed grasp. He glanced around the room of his small one-bedroom apartment. His eyes fell on the pictures of his children as their laughter echoed in his mind. His life seemed stitched together with threads of heartache and loneliness. From his earliest memories, Paul had always felt like an outsider in his own family. His parents, stern and distant, seldom offered him the warmth and affection he craved. They doted on his younger brother, Daniel, whose every achievement was celebrated, while Paul's efforts were met with indifference or criticism.

As a child, Paul would often find solace in the library, burying himself in books where he imagined living the lives of heroes who were loved and cherished. He hoped that one day, his parents would see his worth, but that day never came. Instead, the gap between him and his family widened, each slight and dismissal carving a deeper wound in his heart.

Years passed, and Paul grew into a quiet, introspective young man. He met a woman named Lily during his college years. She was vibrant and full of life, everything he wasn't but wished to be. For a brief period, He believed he had found his sanctuary in her. They married, and he envisioned a future where the love he missed from his family would be found in his new one.

But even Lily, with her infectious laughter and bright spirit, grew distant over time. She found Paul's quiet nature irritating; his introspection boring. She yearned for excitement, for the kind of spontaneity that Paul could never provide. Their home, once filled with hope, turned cold. Conversations became rare, and when they did happen, they were laced with sarcasm and frustration. Paul would lie awake at night, staring at the ceiling, wondering what he had done wrong, why his love wasn't enough.

Their children, two beautiful daughters, and a handsome son were Paul's pride and joy. He poured all his love into them, hoping to shield them from the rejection he had faced. But as they grew older, influenced by their mother's perspective of their father, they too began to see Paul as irrelevant. He was the shadow in the corner, the quiet presence they could easily ignore. His attempts to connect with them were met with eye rolls and sighs, and eventually, even those interactions ceased.

Paul's brother, Daniel, had grown into a successful man, with a family that adored him. Whenever Paul attended family gatherings, he felt like an intruder. His parents and Daniel would share stories and laughter, while Ethan sat on the periphery, a silent observer in a life he should have been part of. The rare times he spoke up, his words would hang awkwardly in the air, unnoticed or quickly dismissed.

As the years dragged on, Paul's heart grew heavier with the weight of rejection. He stopped trying to reach out, the fear of further rejection paralyzing him. He withdrew into himself, finding solace in the company of books and the faint memories of a time when he believed he could be loved. He walked through life like a ghost, invisible to those who mattered most to him.

One cold winter evening, as the snow fell gently outside, Paul sat alone in his small, dimly lit apartment. The silence was deafening, a stark reminder of the void in his life. He picked up an old family photo, the edges worn from years of holding it, and traced the faces with his fingers. Tears welled up in his eyes, and he whispered into the empty room, "Why wasn't I enough?"

As the night deepened, he realized he had been

searching for love and acceptance in the wrong places. He understood that the rejection he faced was not a reflection of his worth, but rather the inability of others to see it. This realization brought a bittersweet comfort. He knew he could never change the past, nor the hearts of those who had turned away from him, but he could find peace within himself.

Paul spent his remaining days in quiet reflection, no longer seeking validation from those who had refused to give it. He embraced his solitude, finding beauty in the silence and strength in his resilience. Though his life had been marred by rejection, He discovered a profound sense of self-acceptance. In the end, he learned that sometimes, the greatest love we can find is the love we give ourselves.

Sammy's World

The summer of 1972 was as blisteringly hot as any other in Claiborne County, Mississippi. The cicadas droned in the thick, humid air, and the sun beat down mercilessly on the red dirt roads wounding through the countryside. In the small town of Prospect, life moved slowly, as if the heat had a tangible weight that slowed everything to a crawl.

Nine-year-old Samuel "Sammy" Johnson stood at the edge of the schoolyard, his small frame casting a long shadow in the late afternoon sun. The other children had already scattered, their laughter echoing faintly as they disappeared down the streets toward their homes. Sammy lingered, his eyes fixed on the ground, kicking at the loose gravel with worn-out shoes.

Sammy dreaded going home. The small, clapboard

house at the end of a dusty road was a place of constant tension and fear. His mother, Ruth, was sickly and frail, often confined to the hospital bed that seemed to swallow her whole. Her absence left a void in the house, a silence filled only by the heavy presence of his father, Earl.

Earl Johnson was a large man, his face weathered and stern. He worked long hours at the local mill, and when he came home, he brought with him an air of exhaustion and frustration that hung over the household like a storm cloud. Sammy had learned to tread lightly around his father, to avoid the sharp words and cold stares that seemed to follow every misstep.

At school, things weren't much better. Sammy was one of the few black students in the predominantly white Prospect Elementary. The other children picked on him relentlessly, their taunts and jeers a constant background noise to his days. Even the teachers seemed to regard him with a mixture of disdain and indifference, their expectations for him low and their patience even lower.

Today had been particularly rough. Mrs. Whitaker, his fourth-grade teacher, had scolded him in front of the class for not finishing his math worksheet. He had tried to explain that he didn't understand the problems, but she had cut him off with a sharp, "That's enough, Samuel. You need to apply yourself more."

The snickers from his classmates had burned in his ears, and he had spent the rest of the day trying to disappear into his seat.

As he walked home, Sammy felt the weight of the day pressing down on him. The road stretched out before him, each step taking him closer to the place he least wanted to be.

He wished he could be anywhere else, wished he could be someone else. But wishes were for dreamers, and Sammy had learned early on that dreams didn't come true for boys like him.

He pushed open the gate to the small yard, the rusty hinges squealing in protest. The house loomed before him, its paint peeling and the windows clouded with grime. He took a deep breath and stepped inside.

The interior was dim, the heavy curtains drawn against the harsh afternoon light. Sammy's eyes took a moment to adjust to the gloom. He could hear the faint hum of the television from the living room, where his father sat in his usual spot, a beer in one hand and a cigarette in the other.

"Is that you, boy?" Earl's voice was a low growl, the words slurred slightly.

"Yes, sir," Sammy replied quietly, slipping off his shoes and setting his school bag down by the door.

"Get in here boy!"

Sammy's heart pounded as he walked into the

living room. Earl's eyes were bloodshot, his face set in a permanent scowl. The room smelled of stale smoke and sweat, a combination that made Sammy's stomach churn.

"How was school?" Earl asked though the question was more of a formality than genuine interest.

"It was fine," Sammy lied, keeping his gaze fixed on the floor.

"Fine, huh?" Earl took a long drag from his cigarette, exhaling slowly. "Mrs. Whitaker called today."

Sammy's heart sank. He knew what was coming next.

"Said you aint payin' attention in class. Said you fallin' behind."

"I'm trying, Daddy," Sammy said, his voice barely above a whisper.

"Tryin' ain't good enough," Earl snapped. "You gotta do betta, boy! You ain't gonna get nowhere in life if you don't start workin' harder!"

Sammy nodded, his throat tight with the effort of holding back tears. He knew better than to cry in front of his father.

"Go on, now. Get your chores done," Earl said, waving him away.

Sammy hurried to the kitchen, his hands shaking as he started on the dishes. The sound of the water running was a small comfort, drowning out the noise of the television and his father's muttered curses.

As he scrubbed the plates and cups, he thought of his mother. Ruth was a gentle soul, her smile a rare but precious gift. When she was home, she tried to shield Sammy from the worst of Earl's temper, but her illness often left her too weak to do much more than offer a few kind words and a comforting hug.

Sammy finished the dishes and moved on to sweeping the floor, his mind wandering as he worked. He imagined a different life, a life where his mother was healthy and his father was kind. He imagined a life where he was just another kid, not the target of everyone's anger and frustration.

But as the sun set and the shadows lengthened, Sammy knew that such a life was as distant and unattainable as the stars that would soon dot the night sky. For now, all he could do was survive, one day at a time, and hope that someday, things might change.

Sundays were the only days that brought Sammy a semblance of peace. The church bells would ring out across the town, calling the faithful to worship. Prospect Baptist Church was a modest white building with a steeple that reached toward the heavens. It was the only black church in town and it was here that Sammy found a brief respite from the harshness of his daily life.

Ruth, despite her illness, insisted on attending church whenever she could. She believed in the power of prayer and the strength of community, and she wanted Sammy to grow up with those same values. Earl, on the other hand, was a man of little faith, often opting to stay home nursing a hangover rather than joining his family in the pews.

That Sunday, Ruth was well enough to go. Sammy helped her get dressed, carefully buttoning her blouse and making sure her hair was neat. Her hands trembled as she fastened her hat, but she smiled at him with a warmth that made his heartache.

"You's a good boy, Sammy," she said softly, patting his cheek. "The Lord watchin' over you, even when it don't seem like it," she said in boken English.

Sammy nodded, though he wasn't sure he believed it. Still, the thought was comforting in its way.

They walked to the church together, Ruth leaning heavily on Sammy's arm. The congregation greeted them with smiles and nods, though there were whispers behind their backs. Everyone knew about Earl's drinking and Ruth's illness, and in a small town like Prospect, gossip traveled fast.

The service was a blur of hymns and sermons, the preacher's voice rising and falling in a rhythm that lulled Sammy into a state of calm. He sat close to his mother, her presence a shield against the world. When it came time for the congregation to bow their heads in prayer, Sammy closed his eyes tightly and wished for strength, for his mother to get better, and for his father to change.

After the service, they lingered outside the church, chatting with the other congregants. Ruth's friends clucked over her like mother hens, expressing their concern and offering help that she politely declined. Sammy stood by her side, silent and watchful.

"How you holdin' up, Sammy?" Mrs. Johnson, an elderly woman with a kind smile, asked him.

"I'm okay, ma'am," he replied, glancing at his mother to make sure she was alright.

"You a brave boy," she said, patting his shoulder. "Your mama's lucky to have you."

Sammy didn't feel brave. He felt small and scared most of the time, but he forced a smile and thanked her.

The walk home was slower, Ruth's energy waning. By the time they reached the house, she was ashen and sweating, and Sammy helped her to the couch, fetching a glass of water and her medication. Earl was still asleep, sprawled out in the recliner, snoring loudly.

"Rest now, Mama," Sammy said, covering her with a light blanket.

"Thank you, baby," she murmured, closing her eyes.

Sammy sat by her side, watching her breathe. He wished he could do more to help her, but he was just a boy, and there were limits to what he could do. The responsibility was heavy on his small shoulders, but he bore it as best he could.

The afternoon stretched out in a languid haze, the quiet broken only by the occasional sound of Earl stirring in his sleep. Sammy read from his schoolbooks, trying to get ahead on his assignments. He was determined to prove Mrs. Whitaker wrong, to show her that he could succeed despite everything.

As evening fell, Ruth woke and smiled at him. "You such a good boy, Sammy," she said again. "Never forget that."

"I won't, Mama," he promised.

And in that moment, surrounded by the shadows of their small home, Sammy held on to those words like a lifeline, a beacon of hope in the darkness surrounding him.

The Little Boy on Side of The Road

The car sputtered and groaned to a halt, steam billowing from the hood. There was no service station for miles. John sighed, cursing his luck, as he pulled over to the side of the deserted country road. Night had fallen, and the vast fields around him were now blanketed by darkness. The nearest town was miles away, and his cell phone sat useless in the passenger seat, the battery long since drained. He'd forgotten his charger and was now paying the price.

Reluctantly, he grabbed his flashlight and stepped out into the cool night air. The flashlight's beam pierced the darkness, illuminating the gravel road stretching ahead. With no other options, John began walking, hoping to find a house where he could use a phone or charge his own. The night was silent and still.

Only his footsteps crunching on the brittle gravel below could be heard.

After what seemed like an eternity, a tiny figure appeared in the distance, moving toward him. As he drew closer, John realized it was a little boy, no older than nine or ten. The boy's appearance was strange—his clothes were old-fashioned, like something from a history book. A worn, woolen cap sat atop his head, and his pants were patched in several places.

"Hey there," John called out, his voice echoing in the stillness. "What are you doing out here all alone?"

The boy didn't respond. Instead, he continued to walk toward John, his expression blank, almost vacant. The way he moved was unnerving as if he were gliding rather than walking. John's discomfort grew as the distance between them gradually closed.

When they were only a few feet apart, John knelt, trying to make himself less intimidating. "Are you lost? Do you need help? Where are your parents?" he asked gently.

The boy stopped and looked at him, his eyes eerily reflecting the flashlight's beam. For a moment, John thought he saw a flicker of sadness—or maybe fear—in the boy's eyes. Then, without a word, the little boy began drifting away across the open field.

John stood up, confused. "Wait!" he called, taking a step after him. "Where are you going?"

The boy didn't look back. He moved steadily across the field, through the tall grass without disturbing a single blade. John watched, frozen in place. He could hardly believe his eyes as the boy's spectral figure became increasingly faint, eventually disappearing into the darkness of night and the mysterious unknown.

As suddenly as he had appeared, the little boy was gone, leaving John alone once more. He stood there with his heart pounding. Silence engulfed him. Then, with a shiver, he turned to the road and continued walking, the memory of the little boy's strange, ghostly figure lingering in his mind.

John never found a house that night, and when he returned to his car at dawn, it started without hesitation. Away he drove, leaving the dark road and its mysteries behind, but the encounter with the little boy would haunt him for years to come. It was a fleeting, inexplicable moment that he would never fully understand, a brush with the unknown that would forever remain shrouded in the shadows of his memory.

The Plan

In the year 2029, the skyline of New Haven dazzled with a blend of modern architectural marvels and historical edifices. Among these, Yale University stood as a bastion of knowledge and discovery, its Gothic spires juxtaposed against sleek research facilities. Dr. Eliza Latham, a tenured professor of molecular biology and a respected researcher, found herself at the center of a disturbing revelation that threatened to upend everything she thought she knew about modern Western medicine, the pharmaceutical industry, and the U.S. food industry.

An unwavering pursuit of truth had always driven Dr. Latham. Even as a child, it was well known by anyone close to her that when she locked on to something, look out!! This was a trait that served her well in her professional life. Her work in genetic epidemiology had garnered international acclaim, but a chance discovery in the university's archives set her on a treacherous path. While researching historical dietary patterns and their impacts on modern diseases, she stumbled upon a collection of old, dusty, forgotten documents stuffed in three large accordion files labeled The Plan. "What plan?" she wondered. She casually opened the first file. As she began to read, she realized these were no ordinary files. This was huge!!

The next three weeks came and went as she poured over the documents in stunned silence. These papers, buried deep within the archives, detailed a clandestine meeting that had taken place in the 1950s between high-ranking executives of major pharmaceutical companies, Healthcare conglomerates, the Food and Drug Administration (FDA), and leaders from the food industry.

The documents were meticulously detailed, outlining a sinister plan to manipulate the public into becoming dependent on unhealthy, addictive foods. The goal was clear: create a population plagued with chronic illnesses such as diabetes and high blood pressure, ensuring a steady stream of profits from all of the major players while the Food and Drug Administration received kickbacks from each sector for looking the other way. The plan also emphasized the importance of developing treatments that only managed symptoms rather than curing diseases, ensuring lifelong customers rather than cured patients.

Dr. Latham's initial reaction was disbelief. How could such a conspiracy remain hidden for over six decades? She didn't want it to be true. But the evidence was irrefutable. The names listed in the documents included some of the most prominent figures in their respective industry at the time, their signatures affixed to a binding agreement. The more she delved into the files, the more connections she uncovered. She found records of financial transactions, secret correspondences, and, most disturbingly, a pattern of unexplained deaths among scientists and doctors who had come too close to the truth.

The names of these deceased professionals read like a who's who of mid-20th century medical pioneers—brilliant minds who had died under mysterious circumstances, their deaths ruled as accidents or suicides. Dr. Latham couldn't shake the feeling that these individuals had been silenced to protect the conspiracy.

Driven by a sense of duty, she decided to dig deeper. She discreetly contacted a few trusted colleagues, sharing her findings and seeking their counsel. Among them was Dr. Michael Chen, a renowned epidemiologist known for exposing corporate wrongdoing. As he reviewed the documents, Dr. Chen's skepticism quickly turned to horror.

"We need to go public with this," Dr. Chen urged. "The world needs to know the truth."

But Dr. Latham was wary. "If we do, we'll be putting ourselves in grave danger. Look at what happened to those who came before us."

Over the next few months, she and Dr. Chen worked secretly, compiling irrefutable evidence to present to the public. They reached out to investigative journalists, preparing a comprehensive exposé. But strange things began to happen as they inched closer to their goal. Dr. Chen's home was broken into, his research files ransacked but nothing stolen. Dr. Latham received anonymous threats, warning her to stop her investigation.

While working late in her lab one evening, Dr. Latham noticed a shadowy figure lurking outside. Her heart raced as she realized the extent of the danger she was in. She doubled down on her security measures, determined to see this through despite the mounting risks.

As the day of the exposé's release approached, she and Dr. Chen felt a mix of fear and exhilaration. They had arranged to meet with a prominent journalist at a secluded location to hand over the final set of documents. But as she made her way to the meeting point, a sense of foreboding washed over her. She couldn't shake the feeling that something was terribly wrong.

When she arrived, the journalist was nowhere to be found. Instead, she found Dr. Chen's lifeless body slumped in his car, a single bullet wound to the head. Panic surged through her as she realized the depths of the conspiracy and the lengths to which those involved would go to protect their secret.

Desperate and alone, she fled, clutching the damning evidence. She knew she couldn't trust anyone, not even the authorities. The conspiracy ran far too deep. The stakes were higher than ever imagined. As she disappeared into the night, her mind raced with unanswered questions and an unrelenting fear for her own life.

The world continued to spin. Life went on, oblivious to the dark machinations at work. As Dr. Latham vanished into the shadows, the truth remained frighteningly close to being buried forever, leaving the American people needlessly ill and at the mercy of an insidious plot conceived by greed.

The Wanderer

In the year 2089, Earth found itself on the brink of a celebration like no other in its history. The scientific community had christened it 'Eventide,' a cosmic spectacle that was predicted to be the most visually stunning celestial event humanity had ever laid eyes on. An enigmatic celestial body, initially mistaken for a rogue planet, had stealthily infiltrated the solar system, hurtling through the Kuiper Belt at an unprecedented velocity and setting its course towards the inner planets. Astronomers were abuzz, governments declared it a global holiday, and people from all corners of the globe braced themselves to witness this once-in-a-lifetime marvel.

In the days leading up to Eventide, excitement reached fever pitch. Telescopes of all sizes were trained on the sky, schools organized field trips to observatories, and millions of people camped in parks and open spaces, eager for an unobstructed view. The unknown celestial body, now referred to as "The Wanderer," was expected to pass close enough to the moon to create a brilliant light show in the night sky.

On the night of the event, the world seemed to hold its breath. Families gathered, friends reunited, and strangers shared a sense of collective awe. As dusk fell, The Wanderer appeared on the horizon, a glowing orb growing steadily larger. People watched in amazement, the air filled with excited chatter and gasps of wonder.

But as the minutes ticked by, the atmosphere of excitement morphed into a cloud of bewilderment. The Wanderer was not adhering to the anticipated pace. Telescopes swiftly recalibrated its trajectory, and in a heartbeat, panic gripped the scientific community. Alarms blared at NASA, the European Space Agency, and every observatory across the globe. This was no ordinary flyby. The Wanderer was hurtling towards the moon at an alarming speed. How could the scientists have miscalculated so gravely?

Attempts to warn the public were futile. Crowds watched in horror as The Wanderer grew larger, its surface details becoming visible to the naked eye. Then, it happened. With a cataclysmic impact, The Wanderer collided with the moon. A blinding flash illuminated the night, turning darkness into day. The ground trembled as shockwaves reverberated through the Earth.

Chaos erupted. Crowds that had been jubilant moments before were now screaming, running in every direction, desperately seeking shelter from an event that offered no escape. In cities, the streets became rivers of terrified humanity. In rural areas, people fled to their homes, wondering where else to turn. But where do you hide from a rogue planet on a collision course with your own?

Them

In the small town of Brooksville, three middle school friends—Jake, Emily, and Carlos—spent countless afternoons in Jake's garage, blending their favorite music genres. Jake, a virtuoso on the guitar, loved jazz. A classical piano prodigy, Emily had a knack for turning Mozart into modern pop. Carlos, the funky bassist with a flair for rhythm, brought the groove. Their fusion of pop, jazz, funk, and classical music was unique, but their band remained nameless.

One evening, after another exhilarating jam session, Emily suggested they launch a worldwide contest to name their band. With the power of social media, they reached out to music lovers across the globe, promising a grand reward to the winner. Billions of submissions poured in, each more imaginative than the last. Yet, the simplicity of "Them," proposed by a 10-year-old girl from France named Sophie, resonated deeply with the trio. "Them" encapsulated the band's essence: a collective of diverse influences coming together to create a sound, a distinctive image, that only a unique name would do. Sophie was made an honorary member of the band and given a generous 1% stake in the band's future earnings.

As "Them," their rise to stardom was meteoric. Their first album, "Symphony of Sound or Simply S.O.S," broke records all over the globe, blending intricate piano sonatas with jazzy guitar riffs and funky bass lines. Audiences were mesmerized, critics were enthralled, and soon, "Them" was a household name. Their concerts were spectacles, drawing crowds in the millions, each show more electrifying than the last.

However, fame came at a cost. Jake, Emily, and Carlos found their lives increasingly restricted. Legions of adoring fans awaited them at every turn, desperate for a glimpse of their idols. Stalkers became a terrifying reality, and the once carefree friends now needed constant security. The loss of their individual freedoms weighed heavily on them, but their passion for music kept them going.

As they prepared for the European leg of their "S.O. S" tour, "Them" boarded a private jet bound for Paris. The excitement was tangible; the world awaited another of their legendary performances. Hours passed, and when the plane was due to land, it never did. Panic spread quickly as search teams scoured the skies and seas.

Days later, the jet's wreckage was discovered in a remote mountainous region. The plane was shattered, but something far more mysterious baffled investigators: there was no trace of Jake, Emily, Carlos, or any of the crew. It was as if they had vanished into thin air. The news of their disappearance sent shockwaves around the world, leaving fans and loved ones in despair.

Rumors and theories abounded. Some claimed the name of their tour, "S.O. S" had been a coded message begging for rescue from some nefarious organization. Others claimed it was a publicity stunt, others believed in extraterrestrial involvement. A few even whispered about a secret island where the band continued to create music away from the world's prying eyes. But the truth remained elusive, shrouded in mystery.

Years passed, and the legend of "Them" grew and entered the realm of myth. Their music continued to inspire new generations, each note echoing the brilliance and enigma of their creators. The world never forgot the band that redefined music and then disappeared without a trace. How could it?

In a small town in France, Sophie, now an adult, often wondered about the band she named. She would play their songs on quiet nights, feeling a connection that transcended time and distance. And sometimes, she thought she could hear a whisper in the music—a secret message, a clue, a promise that somewhere, somehow, "Them" was still out there, playing the soundtrack of their extraordinary lives.

Tony Parker

He sat slumped in his seat. The cracked vinyl cushion did nothing to soften the harsh reality of his Brown Hall nightmare. Brown Hall was the name of the building where first-year students went for remedial classes. He had no problem passing his English class, but math was another story entirely. It was a language he desperately needed and wanted to learn, but it seemed impossible. He found himself stuck in this endless cycle of humiliation and shame. He felt dumb and out of place. To say that he hated Brown Hall was a major understatement. Even the sight of the building conjured emotions he wished he didn't feel. The fluorescent lights above buzzed incessantly, adding to his growing frustration. Every time the professor scribbled an equation on the chalkboard, Tony's heart sank a little deeper. The numbers seemed to mock him, rearranging themselves into impossible puzzles and patterns simply to spite him.

Each class began the same way. He would stare at the board with a determined expression, but his resolve slowly crumbled as the minutes ticked. He watched as other students came and went, their expressions ranging from smug cockiness to resigned acceptance. Every departure felt like another blow to his already fragile self-esteem.

"Parker, you need to pay attention," Professor Harding's sharp and unsympathetic voice cut through his thoughts. "This isn't high school anymore," she said.

Tony's cheeks burned with humiliation. He nodded, eyes downcast, and forced himself to focus. But the numbers swam before his eyes, merging into an incomprehensible blur. He was stuck in a loop of frustration and self-doubt, unable to break free.

One by one, his classmates found ways to escape the drudgery of remedial math. Some moved on to higher-level courses, others dropped the class for different reasons, and a few simply vanished without explanation. Tony envied them all. Every time a seat was left vacant, he felt the crushing weight of his own inadequacy.

Days turned into weeks, weeks into months, and months into years. Tony's grades continued to plummet, and the once faint whispers of doubt grew louder. He spent sleepless nights poring over textbooks, but the numbers refused to give up their secrets. His roommates, immersed in their own studies and social lives, barely noticed his struggle.

One rainy afternoon, Tony trudged through the campus, his footsteps echoing the hollow feeling inside him. He paused by the library, staring at the imposing building. It had always been a place of refuge for him, but now it felt like a prison. The thought of another semester in Brown Hall was unbearable.

With a heavy heart, Tony made his way to the administration building. The decision to drop out of college had been brewing for weeks, but now it felt inevitable. He could no longer endure the daily humiliation, the relentless reminder of his mathematical shortcomings.

As he filled out the paperwork, Tony's mind drifted. What would his future look like without a degree? The uncertainty gnawed at him, but it was preferable to the torment of his current reality. He handed the completed form to the administrator; her impassive expression gave no indication of judgment.

Leaving the building, Tony felt a strange mix of relief and fear. The campus seemed different now as if it had already moved on without him. Aimlessly, he wandered, unsure of where to go next. The rain had intensified, drenching him to the bone, but he barely noticed.

Lost in thought, Tony found himself at the edge of the campus, near a construction site for a new science building. He stood there, watching the machinery move with mechanical precision, a stark contrast to his own chaotic life. The rain pounded the Earth, creating muddy rivulets that snaked across the ground.

Suddenly, a flash of light caught his eye. At first, he thought it was a reflection from the machinery, but as he looked closer, he saw a shimmering portal, like a tear in the fabric of reality. It pulsed with an otherworldly glow, beckoning him.

Tony hesitated, his rational mind grappling with the impossible sight before him. But something deep inside urged him forward. He took a tentative step, then another, until he stood directly in front of the portal. The air around it hummed with energy, sending a thrill through his body.

Tony touched the portal's edge without fully understanding why. The world around him dissolved into a kaleidoscope of colors, and he felt himself being pulled into a new dimension.

He found himself in a vast, otherworldly landscape when the swirling colors subsided. The sky was deep indigo streaked with silver clouds, and the ground beneath his feet glowed with a soft, bioluminescent light. Strange, ethereal beings floated past, their forms shifting and changing like liquid.

Tony took a deep breath, feeling a sense of calm wash over him. Here, in this alien realm, the burdens of his past life seemed to fall away. The beings around him regarded him with curious yet compassionate eyes. One of them approached, its voice resonating in his mind rather than his ears.

"Welcome, Tony. You have been chosen for a purpose beyond your understanding. Here, you will find the knowledge you seek and, perhaps, something even greater."

Tony's heart raced, but it was with excitement rather than fear for the first time in a long while. He nodded, ready to embrace whatever this new world had to offer. As he followed the being into the unknown, the portal behind him flickered and vanished, leaving the campus—and his old life—far behind.

Back on Earth, rumors began to circulate about Tony Parker's mysterious disappearance. Some said he had simply run away, unable to cope with the pressures of college life. Others whispered of strange phenomena, portals, and other dimensions. The truth remained elusive, shrouded in mystery and speculation.

In the end, Tony's story became a legend, a

cautionary tale told to new students about the perils of giving up. But somewhere, in a realm beyond comprehension, Tony embarked on a journey that would change him forever, his fate intertwined with the mysteries of the universe.

www.ingramcontent.com/pod-product-compliance
Lightning Source LLC
Chambersburg PA
CBHW072049150726
47996CB00015B/2246